Little Bub

(AND OTHER STORIES)

BY KAREN PETERSON

ILLUSTRATED BY BRANDON HAYMAN

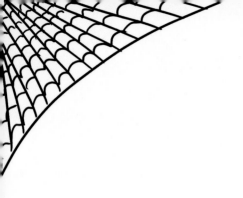

This is a work of fiction. Names, characters,
places and incidents either are the product of the
author's imagination or are used fictitiously, and any
resemblance to any actual persons, living or dead,
events, or locales is entirely coincidental.

To order additional copies of this book, contact:
Xlibris
844-714-8691
www.Xlibris.com
Orders@Xlibris.com

ISBN: Softcover   978-1-6698-7424-9
        EBook   978-1-6698-7423-2

Print information available on the last page

Rev. date: 04/18/2023

Under Lucky Lenny's Bridge

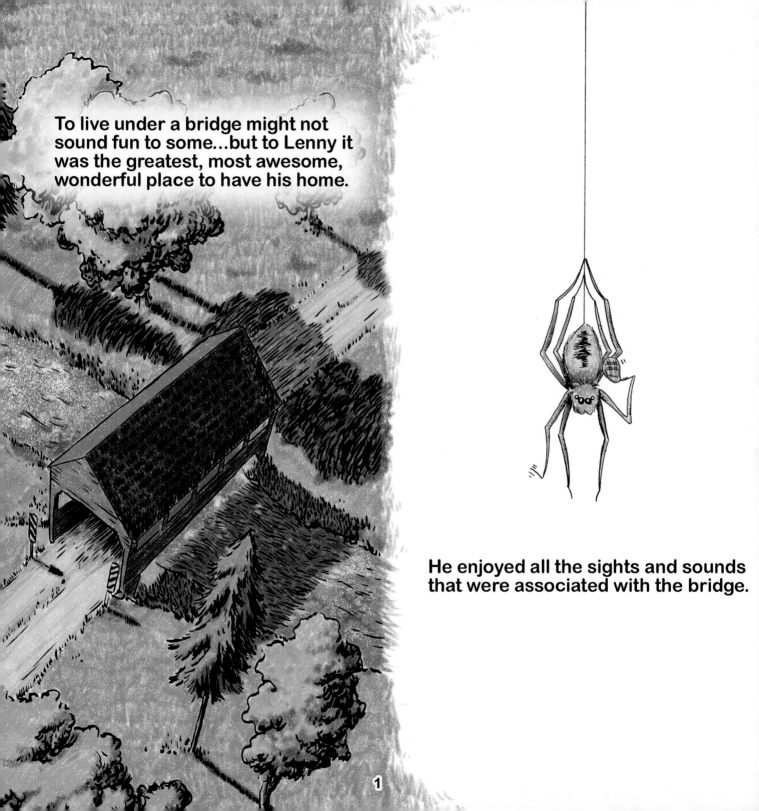

To live under a bridge might not sound fun to some...but to Lenny it was the greatest, most awesome, wonderful place to have his home.

He enjoyed all the sights and sounds that were associated with the bridge.

1

Lenny adored all his friendly neighbors and enjoyed watching and being impressed with such ability to carry bits of mud to create little swallow houses, that soon became homes for countless bird families.

And, not many were so lucky to watch timid deer cautiously appear at the forest edge...then wade into the babbling brook for a refreshing drink of clear water.

Frequently an entire skunk family would wander haphazardly over...then under the bridge.

Some days it was a sweet, nice visit...some not so sweet OR nice at all!

Lenny always delighted when Purr the cat scooted by chasing a butterfly or anything unfortunate enough to catch his attention.

Purr loved to run and jump and play tag with everybody... but not everyone loved it when Purr would run after, jump over, or played tag with them!

The schools of fish came by daily to enjoy the cooling waters beneath the bridge during the hot summer heat. They delighted in diving deep to the chilliest depths to see just how cold it really was and who was silly enough to stay there the longest!

Most days the turtles could be found either lounging on the bank or floating in the energizing water within Lenny's sight. He would call out to them in welcome and daily they all engaged in interesting conversation together.

A fun time was always happening when the children came to play under the shelter of the bridge. Some days they brought a picnic basket filled with yummy smelling food and brightly colored lemonade, that made them squish up their face and give a little shiver when sipped, all the while reaching for the tart drink again and again!

The friends would sit and eat, then wade in the invigorating chilled water, splashing each other and anything that got close enough to be a target to get soaked. They always shared laughter and enjoyed being under the bridge as much as Lenny did.

6

Lenny had no desire to spin a web and float wherever it might take him, as his many brothers and sisters did. Living under the bridge was the most wonderful place on Earth, in Lenny's mind. To be so fortunate to have a beautiful home, friendly neighbors and always a parade of friends stopping by. What more could a spider ask for?

How lucky could one be to live in such a friendly, happy, perfect place as under the bridge!

TEX
AND HIS
SANDCASTLE

Tex awoke to a bright sunshiny day on his sandy little piece of Galveston paradise to the screeches and squawks of his neighbors pestering shell seekers and fishermen for a bite of their tasty snacks. They always enjoyed hovering overhead, not very patiently, hoping for a morsel to be handed over or flung in the air for them to compete for. Most of Tex's friends were timid, quiet neighbors but obviously not these, and that always brought a big cheerful grin to his sweet little face.

Every morning Tex loved to stroll along the water's edge, calling out "Good morning y'all... Howdy!" to the many that live on his beloved beautiful Sandcastle Beach. Tex enjoyed his beach friends and found them all very loveable and considered himself lucky to know them!

Tex looked forward and loved the season on his soft sandy beach when the many gazillion vacationers came to play on the sand or splash in the gentle salty waves. He adored the laughter and squeals of delight from sandy, salty, sunburned families enjoying time together and having yummy looking picnics.

And by the way...so did the seagull neighbors!

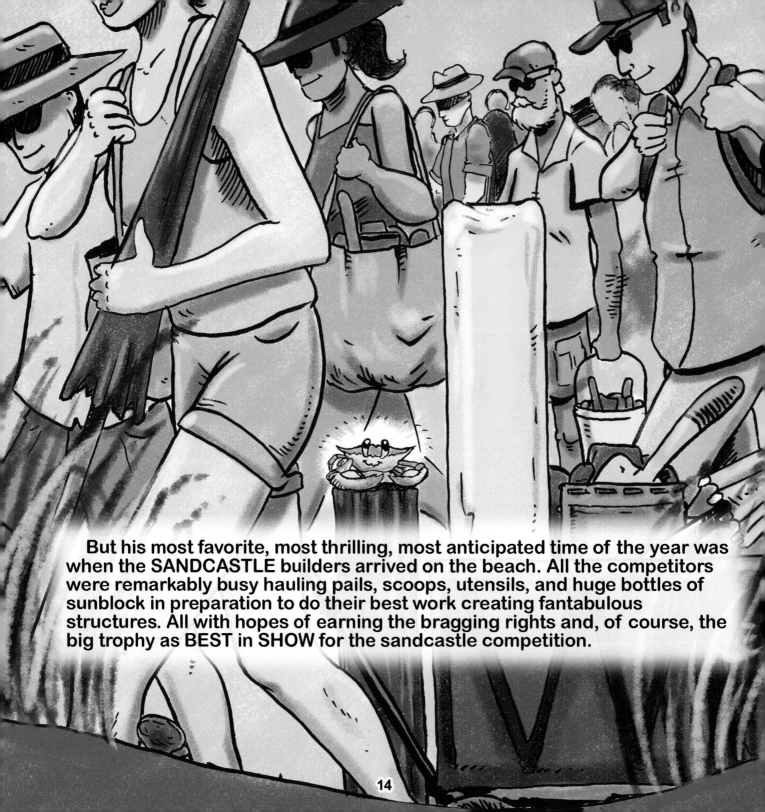

But his most favorite, most thrilling, most anticipated time of the year was when the SANDCASTLE builders arrived on the beach. All the competitors were remarkably busy hauling pails, scoops, utensils, and huge bottles of sunblock in preparation to do their best work creating fantabulous structures. All with hopes of earning the bragging rights and, of course, the big trophy as BEST in SHOW for the sandcastle competition.

Their talent was remarkable to Tex and he loved touring each and every design that was created. He was a little bit unsure if he could construct a mighty-fine sandcastle, just like the competitors did. But as of yet, he had not tried...although each year Tex decided NEXT year was the time to join in, even though he did not have the confidence in himself that he could do it.

Maybe he should start to practice immediately and decide which style he liked best...a monstrous castle, a humongous plate of pancakes, a big waterfall, or even a mother hen and her chicks.

Hmmmmmmm. He would have to think this over and test his skills first, he decided.

Tex was overly excited to become a part of this wonderous, terrific, anticipated event. He had thought about it, researched, and practiced for a long time. And he was ready! The official start day could not come fast enough for him!

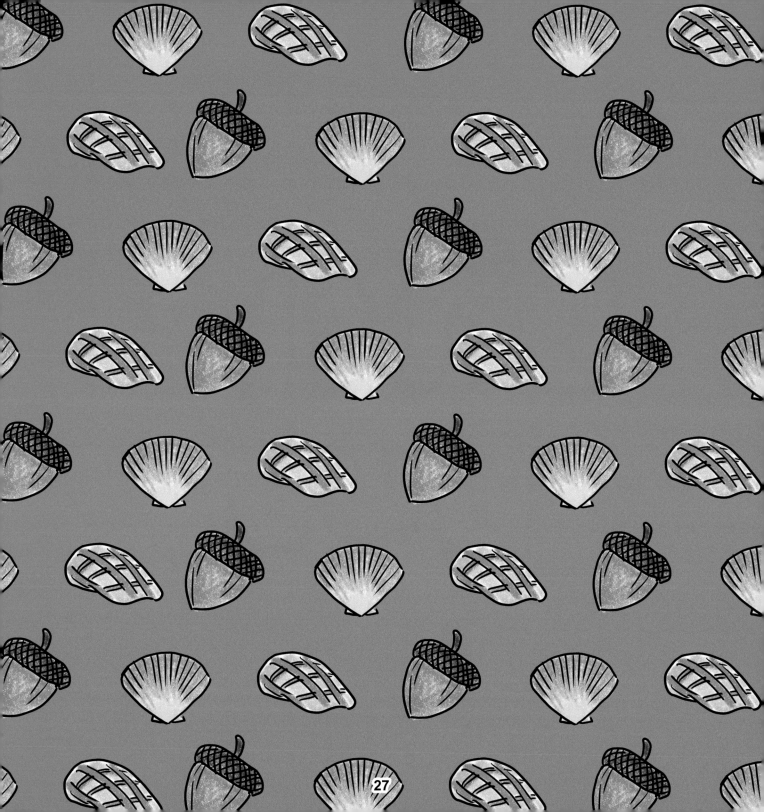

Little Bub was born in a very loving and happy nest with a brother and some wild and crazy sister squirrels. Never a dull moment in their little world.

Each day Mama squirrel was a tireless teacher...preparing her pups with wisdom and choices to care for themselves, build their own nests, and, especially, how to find and harvest plenty of food for wintertime. This proved quite the challenge at times since some of the pups preferred to nap or chase each other tirelessly round the tree trunk.

Before the blink of an eye, time arrived for the young squirrels to make the change from Mama squirrel's nest to their very own Home Sweet Home Nest.

What a HUGE, exciting day for the brothers and sisters...all had ideas just where they wanted to create their own personal dwellings and forage for their winter stockpiles. That is, all but Little Bub.

Of all Mama's squirrel pups, Bub just wanted to have fun and play or lay in the warm sunshine on a branch high in the pecan tree. He had trouble listening and paying attention during class, but figured at the time it did not pertain to him especially! Little did he realize how important all Mama's information would be one day and how he would wish he were back in class hearing all her tips and knowledge!

One cool crisp morning, Little Bub awoke and reality set in! A slight nip in the air? He kinda remembered Mama speaking about this situation. "Hummm, what was it she said? Oh my, I remember now! Mama said, 'We must gather food, so we have plenty to eat when there is snow on the ground and no food to be found!'"

Little Bub knew what he should do for the next few days. He must begin to gather nuts for wintertime, but where did Mama say to put them?

With a burst of energy, Little Bub scampered tree to tree gathering nuts and storing them.

Next day he gathered even more. "What an awesome storage space!"

"WOW! How easy can this be? Storage places are all over the world!"

"Next year, I will know exactly what NOT to do!" whispered the sad and hungry Little Bub.

Printed in the United States
by Baker & Taylor Publisher Services